Old Cricket

LISA WHEELER

Old Cricket

ILLUSTRATIONS BY

PONDER GOEMBEL

ALADDIN PAPERBACKS

NEW YORK LONDON TORONTO SYDNEY

ALADDIN PAPERBACKS
An imprint of Simon & Schuster Children's Publishing Division
1230 Avenue of the Americas, New York, NY 10020
Text copyright © 2003 by Lisa Wheeler
Illustrations copyright © 2003 by Ponder Goembel
ALADDIN PAPERBACKS and colophon are trademarks of Simon & Schuster, Inc.
Also available in an Atheneum Books for Young Readers hardcover edition.
Designed by Michael Nelson
The text of this book was set in Kennerley.
The illustrations for this book were rendered in acrylic paint.
Manufactured in China
First Aladdin Paperbacks edition June 2006
4 5 6 7 8 9 10

The Library of Congress has cataloged the hardcover edition as follows:
Wheeler, Lisa, 1963–
Old Cricket / Lisa Wheeler ; illustrated by Ponder Goembel.
p. cm.
Summary: Old Cricket doesn't feel like helping his wife and neighbors to prepare for winter and so he pretends to have all sorts of ailments that require the doctor's care, but hungry Old Crow has other ideas.
ISBN-13: 978-0-689-84510-9 (hc.)
ISBN-10: 0-689-84510-3 (hc.)
[1. Crickets—Fiction. 2. Crows—Fiction. 3. Helpfulness—Fiction. 4. Behavior—Fiction.]
I. Goembel, Ponder, ill. II. Title
PZ7.W5657 Ol 2003
[Fic]—dc21   2002002199
ISBN-13: 978-1-4169-1855-4 (Aladdin pbk.)
ISBN-10: 1-4169-1855-8 (Aladdin pbk.)

For two terrific in-laws,
Carol Wheeler (who is no dumb bug)
and Bob Wheeler, who has fixed
a few roofs in his day
Love, L. W.

For D. J.
—P. G.

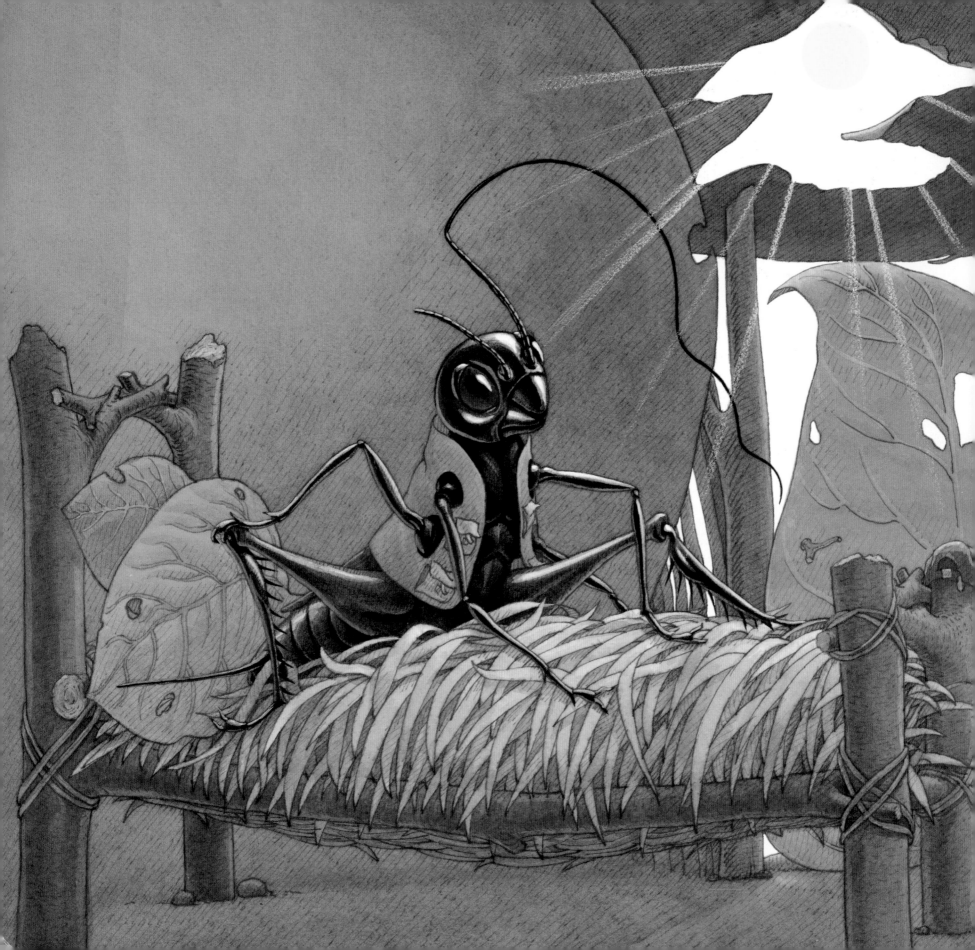

Old Cricket woke up
feeling cranky.
And crotchety.
And cantankerous.

So when his missus asked him to
ready their roof for winter, he came up
with a clever plan. (You don't get to be
an *old* cricket by being a dumb bug.)

"Consarn it!" he cried. "I woke
with a creak in my knee, dear wife.
I can't be climbing rooftops today."

"Well, hobble yourself over to see
Doc Hopper," she ordered, and bundled
up a bit of breakfast for him to eat
along the way.

Old Cricket took his bundle and
left the house with a *creak-creak-creak,*
in case his missus was watching.

He hadn't gone far when he came upon his cousin, Katydid, who was picking berries off a bush for winter.

"Good to see you, Cousin," said Katydid. "Have you come to help me pick berries?"

Old Cricket, still feeling cranky, didn't want to help. So he came up with a clever plan. (You don't get to be an *old* cricket by being a dumb bug.)

"I wish I could," said Old Cricket. "But I woke
with a creak in my knee and a crick in my neck,
so I can't pick berries today. I'm off to see
Doc Hopper."

"That's too bad," said Cousin Katydid.
"Here, have a berry to munch along
the way."

Old Cricket packed the berry in his
bundle with his breakfast. Then he
wobbled off with a *creak-creak-creak*,
and a *crick-crick-crick*, in case Katydid
was watching.

When the sun was high in the sky, Old Cricket saw his neighbors, the Ants, in their field. They were bringing in the last of the corn.

"Wonderful to see you," said Uncle Ant. "Have you come to help with the harvest?"

Old Cricket, still feeling crotchety, didn't want to help. So he came up with a clever plan. (You don't get to be an *old* cricket by being a dumb bug.)

"I'm sorry," said Old Cricket. "But I woke with a creak in my knee, a crick in my neck, and a crack in my back. I can't haul corn today. I'm off to see Doc Hopper."

"That's too bad," said Uncle Ant. "Here, take a small kernel to nibble along the way."

Old Cricket packed the kernel into his bundle with his berry and his breakfast. Then he dawdled off with a *creak-creak-creak*, and a *crick-crick-crick*, and a *crack-crack-crack*, in case Uncle Ant was watching.

Now Old Cricket, tired from carrying the bulging
bundle but feeling rather pleased with his clever self, had
no intention of going to see Doc Hopper. Instead he
settled under a piney shrub and soon fell fast asleep.

"*Caw-caw-caw!*" He was awakened by Old Crow, who came calling at mealtime. "Have you come to be my lunch?"

Old Cricket, still feeling rather cantankerous, didn't want to be Old Crow's lunch. So he came up with a clever plan. (You don't get to be an *old* cricket by being a dumb bug.)

"I'm sorry," said Old Cricket. "But I woke with a creak in my knee, a crick in my neck, a crack in my back, and a hic-hic-hiccup in my head. I'd surely go bouncing around in your belly if you ate me up today."

Then Old Cricket started off with a *creak-creak-creak*, and a *crick-crick-crick*, and a *crack-crack-crack*, and a *hic-hic-hic*, because he *knew* Old Crow was watching.

But Old Crow was not tricked.
(You don't get to be an old crow by
being a birdbrain.) In a single swoop he
snuck up behind Old Cricket, and . . . CAW . . .
scared some real hiccups right into that dumb bug.

"Now be a good lunch and hold still,"
said Old Crow.

Holding still was the last thing Old
Cricket wanted to do. With his bundle on
his back, he hightailed it toward home with a
hic-hic-hic—and a *caw-caw-caw* close behind.

Hurrying back through the now-empty field, he slipped on strands of cornsilk and . . . WHACK . . . got a crack in his back.

"Cornsakes!" cried Old Cricket, struggling to his feet.

But just before Old Crow could snatch him up, Old Cricket reached into his bundle, pulled out the corn kernel, and tossed it.

Old Crow caught the kernel, but kept on coming.

Old Cricket ran with a *hic·hic·hic* and a *crack·crack·crack*—and a *caw·caw·caw* close behind.

Scurrying past the now-empty
berry bush, he stumbled on a stick
and . . . *THWICK* . . . got a crick in
his neck.

"Crikey!" cried Old Cricket,
scrambling to get away.

But before Old Crow could
gobble him down, Old Cricket
reached into his bundle, plucked
out the berry, and tossed it.

Old Crow caught the berry, but
kept on coming.

Old Cricket ran with a *hic·hic·hic*, and a *crack·crack·crack*, and a *crick·crick·crick*—and a *caw·caw·caw* close behind.

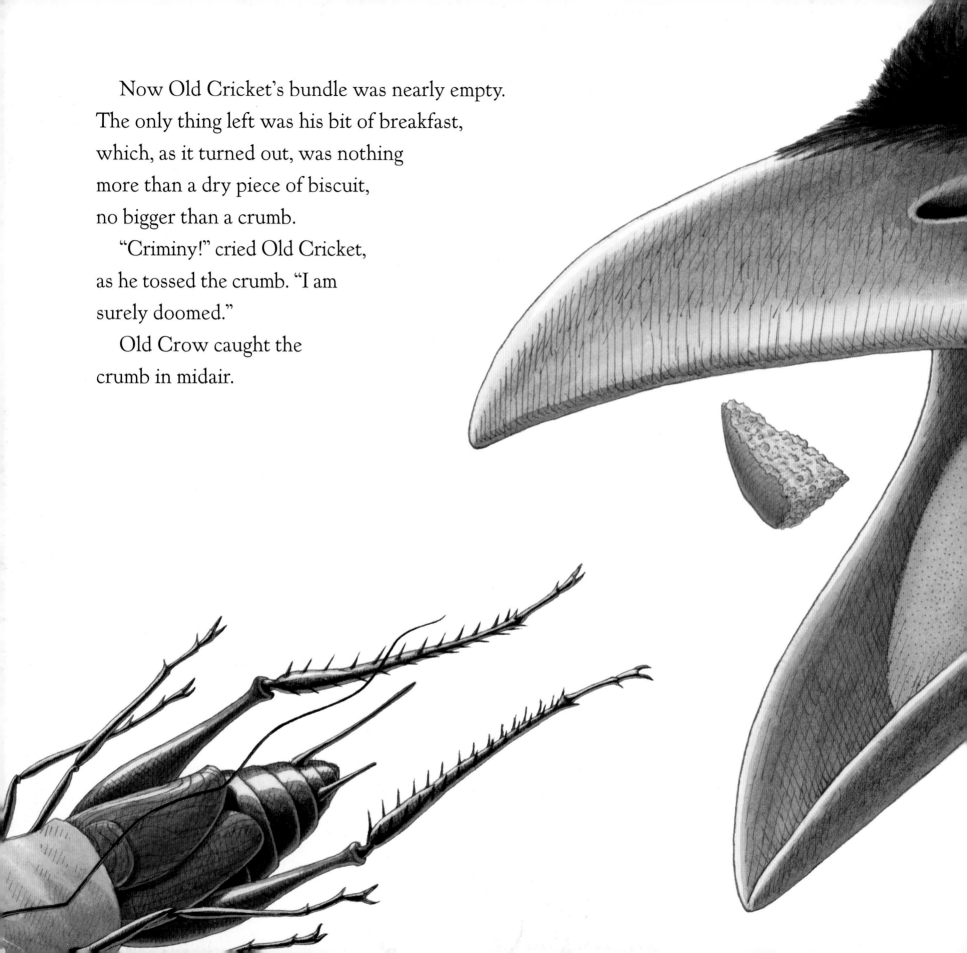

Now Old Cricket's bundle was nearly empty.
The only thing left was his bit of breakfast,
which, as it turned out, was nothing
more than a dry piece of biscuit,
no bigger than a crumb.

"Criminy!" cried Old Cricket,
as he tossed the crumb. "I am
surely doomed."

Old Crow caught the
crumb in midair.

Old Cricket kept on running, with a *hic·hic·hic*,
and a *crack·crack·crack*, and a *crick·crick·crick*, and
now a *creak·creak·creak* coming from his weary knees.

But there was no *caw-caw-caw* close behind.

Instead there came a new sound—a *caw-caw* coughing sound. That crumb had caught smack in the middle of Old Crow's throat!

Old Cricket never slowed as he looked back to see Old Crow, in a flurry of feathers, shaking his claw and *caw-caw* coughing his fool head off.

And as luck would have it, Old
Cricket ran himself out right in front
of Doc Hopper's doorway. Doc Hopper
fixed each *creak*, each *crick*, each *crack*,
and each *hic*. Then he sent Old Cricket
on home where . . .

. . . his missus was waiting with a crook in her finger as she pointed her clever husband toward their sagging rooftop.

('Cause you don't get to be an *old* missus by being a dumb bug.)